Nehemiah Adams

God is Love

SALZWASSER
VERLAG

Nehemiah Adams

God is Love

Reprint of the original.

1st Edition 2023 | ISBN: 978-3-37514-768-6

Verlag (Publisher): Salzwasser Verlag GmbH, Zeilweg 44, 60439 Frankfurt, Deutschland
Vertretungsberechtigt (Authorized to represent): E. Roepke, Zeilweg 44, 60439 Frankfurt, Deutschland
Druck (Print): Books on Demand GmbH, In de Tarpen 42, 22848 Norderstedt, Deutschland

Number Four.

Truths for the Times.

GOD IS LOVE.

A

SUPPLEMENT TO THE AUTHOR'S DISCOURSE

ON THE

Reasonableness of Future, Endless Punishment.

WITH A BRIEF NOTICE OF

REV. T. S. KING'S TWO DISCOURSES

IN REPLY TO SAID DISCOURSE.

BY

NEHEMIAH ADAMS, D. D.,

PASTOR OF THE ESSEX STREET CHURCH, BOSTON

BOSTON:

GOULD AND LINCOLN,

59 WASHINGTON STREET.

NEW YORK: SHELDON, BLAKEMAN & CO.

CINCINNATI: GEORGE S. BLANCHARD.

1858.

ADVERTISEMENT.

HAVING preached a Lecture on "The Reasonableness of Future, Endless Punishment," at his regular Sabbath evening service, and, the next Sabbath evening at Hollis Street Church, by invitation, the author was led to preach a lecture, of which the following pages are the substance, in his own pulpit, at his next Sabbath evening service, with a view to complete his statement of a subject which could not be fully set forth in one discourse. It was originally designed to be printed, but with no reference to any reply, from any source, to the previous lecture,— no such reply having, to the writer's knowledge, then been made.

The pastor of the Hollis Street Church having since published two sermons in reply to the one first named, it will not be thought improper if the present publication should contain, in an appendix, a brief notice of the same. In the discourse itself, however, of which these pages are the substance, the author finds that he had anticipated many things in the "Two Discourses" from Hollis Street, before he knew that they had been preached.

GOD IS LOVE.

WHATEVER may be the component parts and qualities of the sun, its prominent characteristics are light and heat, and all its parts and qualities combine to produce them.

So every thing in God conspires to one thing. That which presides over all his actions, and rules in all his feelings, and pervades his whole nature, so as to give its character, in the view of intelligent beings, to all which he is, and to all which he does, is Love.

It might have been something else; for example, Justice. Whatever we heard, or saw, or felt, of the Most High, might have produced this chief impression upon us, — that God is Just. Or it might have been Power, illustrated in the works of nature, and in his dealings with his creatures. Or it might have been, in a word, Holiness, — every thing conspiring to produce, with an overwhelming impression, the feeling that God is Holy. All these attributes are essential to our reverence and love for God; but these, singly or altogether, are not so preëminently his characteristic, that it can be said with truth, God is Justice, God is Power, God is Holiness.

No one has failed to think what an infinitely solemn thing it is that we live under the absolute disposal of one Being who made us, ordains our lot, and is able to do with us that which seems good in his sight. The question will arise, What security have I for my welfare? Annihilation is impossible. There are elements around me which I cannot control. The wind can destroy me; the chemical combinations in the atmosphere can take away my health, my life; lightnings may consume me; the earth can swallow me up. My disembodied spirit being still susceptible of pleasure and pain, what protection have I in a future state? how do I know that existence, on the whole, will be a blessing, and not a curse? The mind longs for a feeling of certainty that benevolence is and will be the law of our being. God is almighty; no one can go from his presence; how may I know that his power will not be employed to make me unhappy forever, let my character be what it may?

The answer to such thoughts and questionings is found in the incontrovertible truth, that the perfections of God are ruled by Love.

But how does it appear that love guides in the divine administration; that, to a competent spectator, who could see the whole scheme of the divine government, it would appear that the motive, the feeling, and the end aimed at, is Love?

If we can establish the following proposition, which it will be a principal object of these pages to do, this question will be settled in every mind. The proposition is this:

IT IS ESSENTIAL TO THE SUCCESS OF THE DIVINE GOVERNMENT OVER FREE AND ACCOUNTABLE BEINGS, THAT LOVE SHOULD RULE IN THE DIVINE PERFECTIONS.

It would plainly be impossible for this world to exist, as things are now constituted, if love did not pervade the perfections of God, and rule in them. If this is made clear, we shall have no difficulty in applying the truth wherever there are intelligent subjects of the divine government.

If love were not the motive and end of the divine Being, it would be necessary to suppose that some other quality would be ; for in the nature of things, every moral being has some ruling motive or governing purpose. We have only to suppose that the governing purpose or feeling in God were something different from love, his object being not to manifest love as his chief end, but to do something else ; for example, to show his power. This, therefore, is the testimony, we will suppose, which is borne by the heavens, earth, and seas — that God is power. All these things, indeed, now testify that God is powerful ; but suppose that, in the same sense in which it is now said that God is love, it should be said, with equal truth, God is power?

To begin with the seas : What would be seen there? Now, benevolence reigns for the most part over the great deep. A thousand fold more ships pass safely over it than are sunk in it ; innumerably more lives are preserved than destroyed there. Men go to sea with the confidence that there will be favorable winds to bear them to any and every part of the globe ; and every day or week vessels arrive in the different ports from northern climes and southern, from the east and west. This is benevolence ; there is power in it ; but chiefly it illustrates the goodness of God.

But take away benevolence, consulting the happiness of man, from its rule in the divine purposes, and let power ascend and govern to the exclusion of benevolence as the great end. Then the object would be to make the four winds show their strength ; the height of waves, the fury of tempests, the roar of ocean, the apparent mingling of sea and sky, would proclaim, God is power. From the fierce Baltic to the typhoons of the Indian Seas, this voice would go forth, — God is power. Few, if any, sails would tempt the winds of heaven; a keel would seldom venture among the waves whose chief office should be to show that God is power, each billow then, like a wandering green mound, denoting that some human form was intombed there. Commerce would cease; parts of the earth would bid each other farewell; for God is power.

How would it be on land? Gigantic forms of rocks would overhang the dwellings of men, which could then be only in valleys, where the chief locomotive power visible would be the wings of eagles, mocking the weakness of imprisoned man. The rain would descend to show its force, not to bless the earth; the rivers would be swift with currents defying human strength and skill; the springs and fountains which now, like a child's hymn, murmur, "God is good," would rise into torrents, and cry, God is power. Vegetation would be excessive, and men would be cumbered under the prodigality of the earth. Nothing would exist as now merely to give pleasure. The greenness which refreshes the eye would assume a dazzling brilliancy, to impress the mind with a sense of power; the hues and fragrance of flowers would be useless; every where strength would supplant beauty; majesty would tread upon the meek and quiet forms of nature; and the awful power of God would compel the fear and adoration which now, involuntarily, arise with mingled love and praise, at the sight of the touching evidence of his goodness. As for the heavens, day unto day would, indeed, utter speech of him, and night unto night would show forth knowledge, but not as now, (in the elliptical but expressive language of the original,) — "no speech; no language; their voice is not heard;" but, on the contrary, the air would be full of varied and awful grandeur both in sights and sounds; and signs in the sun, moon, and stars would make the nations pale; the grateful vicissitudes of seasons would be exchanged for demon-

strations of omnipotence; the only impression on the minds
of men would be that which is made by the forlorn Moslem
cry through all Mahometan deserts, and seas, and cities,
"God is great."

But let us suppose that the justice of God should make the
predominant impression upon our minds. Then, the world
would be a palace of justice; every place of assembly and
every dwelling would be like a court room; every where we
should see the signs and ministrations of law. Then every
transgression and disobedience would meet with a just recompense of reward. The common spectacle in the streets
would be people meeting with their deserved fate, vengeance seizing on the wicked and mixing for them her cup of
trembling in exact proportion to their crimes. In the midst
of festivity and domestic peace, the sentence of death would
be uttered by ministers of justice, refusing respite or reprieve;
the great end of God's administration of the world would be
to do justice, and to impress a sense of his justice upon men;
the terrors of law and of violated obligation would take the
place of clemency, and the providence of God, which now
makes the sun to rise on the evil and on the good, and sends
rain on the just and the unjust, would be armed on every side
with admonitions of guilt, and of approaching or instant
retribution. Then the softening influences of contrition and
repentance would be exchanged for fear and despair. True,
goodness would meet with its just reward; every righteous
act would be duly paid for, every kind deed be recompensed
at once; but, in that case, virtue would lose the powerful
excitements which disappointment and injury afford; faith,
with its precious influence on the mind and heart, would dis-
appear; probation, that means of spiritual benefit, the divine
method of educating us for a nobler state of existence, would
become impossible; for pure justice would dispense her

rewards immediately, without forbearance towards the wicked, or benevolent delay for the sake of strengthening, and so in the highest measure rewarding, the good. It is evident, therefore, that justice, on which, nevertheless, the safety of the universe depends, could not properly be the governing purpose in the divine mind and administration.

But can the same objections be made to holiness, as the predominant manifestation in the divine character? Yes; even now, while the goodness of God attempers the insufferable rays of his holiness to the eyes of angels and men, the powerful impressions of it are more than they can bear. Angels veil their faces while they worship. In the temple, the cherubim had more wings with which to cover themselves than to fly, while they cried one to another, Holy, holy, holy, is the Lord God of Hosts. At which voice, and under a sense of the holiness of God, Isaiah cried, " Woe is me, for I am undone, because I am a man of unclean lips, and I dwell in the midst of a people of unclean lips, for mine eyes have seen the King, the Lord of Hosts." If the holiness of God should universally make the first predominating impression upon the minds of his creatures whenever they approach him, or think of him, and this impression should be such that no sense of his infinite benevolence mingling with it could mitigate or qualify it, the fear which is cast out by love would occupy every mind; the holiness of God would dazzle the sight beyond endurance ; worship would consist only in distant prostration, nor would any creature, even the archangel, venture to say, "Beloved, now are we the sons of God." A sense of his excellency would make them always afraid. Job said, " Only do not two things unto me ; then will I not hide myself from thee ; withdraw thine hand from me, and let not thy dread make me afraid. Then call thou, and I will answer ; or let me speak, and answer thou me."

But now we see a pleasing contrast to such representations of the divine character. The methods by which God manifests himself to us so as to produce the greatest and best effect upon our moral sense, and thereby to give us the most exalted views of his greatness, are illustrated, for example, in the causes by which light is ordained to give us comfort and pleasure. Power and wisdom are employed in doing it, and yet benevolence is more conspicuous in it than they. The different colors of things are owing to certain qualities in the things themselves, a leaf being constructed so as to reflect green rays, the atmosphere a soft blue; that which we call the color of an object being the result of its construction by the hand of God, who makes the leaves in the woods such that when they decay they gratify us with the variety of their colors. Here the power of God puts forth benevolence as its illustration. It would not have been as great a proof of power so to have made every thing in the air, earth, and sea, that it should absorb all the colors; then nothing would be seen but that which was white, and the sun, with his full splendors reflected from every point, would, with our present eyesight, have been our sore tormentor. Or creation, by some similar process, might have been shrouded in black, and "Night, from her ebon throne," would have stretched her sceptre into the day. While God has chosen to gratify our sense by a benevolent arrangement which makes different objects, and the same objects at different times, shed different rays upon us, his power is more signally illustrated through his benevolence than it could have been by overwhelming impressions of his omnipotent force.

If, therefore, it appears probable that the present state of things, and the happiness of intelligent beings every where, could not exist unless benevolence took the lead in the manifestations of the divine character, we may argue, from the necessity of the case, that if there be a God, love must pervade his perfections and rule in his acts. This is true in those states of society where the true God has not been and is not recognized. "Nevertheless, he left not himself without witness, in that he did good, and gave us rain from heaven, and fruitful seasons, filling our hearts with food and gladness." The heathen and pagan world could not exist, except as the benevolence of God countervailed its constant tendency to self-destruction. "His tender mercies are over all his works." "The earth is full of the goodness of the Lord." "So is this great and wide sea." Intelligent men concur in the acknowledgment that the attributes of God are guided by benevolence, and that there is an evident design in the constitution of things to make this conciliating impression upon the minds of men, that God is good.

Now there is one principal objection which is urged against this view of the divine character. It is drawn from the moral condition of our race. Our fallen nature, our entrance into the world with a moral constitution predisposed to evil, is held to be a sufficient refutation of all proofs of God's goodness drawn from the works of nature. They are inanimate; they promote, it is said, the temporary comfort of man as a necessary means of sustaining life; but here are moral beings in a world blasted by sin, they themselves possessing a sinful nature; — is not such a nature a reproach to the character of the Being who presides over it? Does it not conflict with the doctrine now maintained, that God is love?

The answer may, without hesitation, be, No; and the proof is abundant and clear.

But let it be plainly understood what it is which we now attempt to show. Not one word is here to be said on that perplexing subject, the existence of sin. But, assuming that the Creator proposes to make free, accountable creatures to inhabit this world,— it will now be attempted to show, that we could not have been more favorably placed under any other system which they who impugn the present constitution of things have ever proposed.

May we not all agree upon this question, Whether it is best that God shall make a universe of intelligent creatures, who shall be entirely free in their choice to love and serve God or not? There shall be no compulsion, no predisposition to sin ; on the contrary, rich experience of the character of God, and of what it is to love and serve him, shall be afforded ; and then his subjects shall decide whether to obey or to sin. Is it best that God shall create such a universe? Considering who he is, and taking into view the infinite blessedness of those whom he shall love, and on whom he will forever bestow all that he can give, as far as they are capable of receiving it, we should all, probably, say, It is infinitely desirable that creation should be peopled as widely as possible with these intelligent, free creatures. The probabilities, we should say, are, that such a Being, once known and loved, will secure the obedience of his subjects, and, if so, the happiness of which they will be capable, no finite mind can conceive. It is worthy of a benevolent God, we should say, to bring such an intelligent universe into being.

They come into existence. Some of them dwell in the immediate presence of God. But there, even there, it appears that some of them, in the exercise of their perfectly free choice, keep not their first estate, but leave their own habitation, and, in so doing, forsake their allegiance to God. They must have had, in heaven, every possible inducement to love and serve God ; but for some fancied good which they did not possess, they renounced their loyalty, they became rebels.

We say nothing about their punishment; we only ask, Have we seen any thing up to this point to impugn the goodness of God? They have become sinners, in the exercise of that freedom with which they were endowed instead of being constituted an intellectual orrery, made to revolve, by force, around a central object, whether they would or no. God was good in making them, and in making them free; in all this God is love. Has their transgression cast any reflection upon his character? It may be said, He could have prevented them from sinning; why leave them at such peril? Would a parent suffer his child to expose himself thus to ruin, if the parent could, by any influence, prevent it? The reply is, Parents govern their children, when they are at years of understanding, by surrounding them with powerful moral restraints and persuasive influences; but there is a certain province in the child's free agency which they do not invade. Even in the case of the redeemed, whose perpetual uprightness the Bible teaches us to believe will be made sure, we cannot suppose that any thing will be done which will in the least intrude upon the consciousness of perfect liberty, or suggest the thought or feeling of restricted freedom. Whether it be just and wise to allow every race of beings to be placed on probation at first, is a question which we have not light enough to discuss at much length; we can only say, that there seems to be no want of benevolence in trying their choice, under a full and explicit disclosure of the consequences which will ensue upon obedience or disobedience. No one can properly say that a fair and full statement of a proposal, with all that will follow its acceptance or rejection, does not acquit him who makes the proposal from all blame if the choice inclines to the wrong side. The bias being as strong towards good as towards evil, and not only so, but being fortified by experience in the happy consequences of uprightness, benevolence is not impeachable, if, in pursuit of some imagined advantage, we forsake our first estate, with all its obligations, and seek a selfish end. Such, so far as we can learn, was the case with angels, and we cannot find just cause of exception in it against the benevolence of God, unless we take the ground that, rather than expose immortal creatures to the liability of losing their happiness forever, even by the exercise of their own intelligent and deliberate choice, it would be better that God should have no creatures but flying fowl, and beasts of the earth, and fishes, who cannot possibly, by choosing wrong, involve themselves in such a calamity as sin. Let the universe be an infinite firmament for suns and planets, and let the only forms of intelligence be mechanical revolutions, in sublime cycles, by unnumbered worlds, which shall be dumb, except as their spheres make music, or the irrational creatures which inhabit them utter their voices; and let their wonderful forms of chemistry and mineralogy illustrate the wisdom of the Creator; but let there be no intelligent creature to behold them, and to love and praise God; let almighty goodness bring every thing else into being except an offspring in his own image, lest, perchance, some of them should choose to forsake him, in the pursuit of fancied good! We confidently say that this is not benevolence; and that it is far from being any impeachment of benevolence for God to make spirits in his own image, and give them liberty to every possible extent, with all its liabilities, and with its privileges and blessings.

Next, let us pursue the illustration in the case of our first parents, without any reference to their posterity. Adam is put on probation as a free, accountable creature. God endows him with every form of blessing; holds converse with him; instructs him fully as to his duty, and the consequences of a right or wrong choice. He puts his obedience to the test, by prohibiting one tree, which was necessary neither to existence

2

nor to happiness, provided man would prefer obedience to God
above every other gratification. In all this, God is love. It
is not a temptation to sin. On the one hand, there are posi-
tive experiences of blessing in uprightness, and promises of
further good; on the other, a most explicit dissuasion from
doing wrong, with a disclosure of the consequences. Man, in
the perfectly free exercise of his own will, eats the forbidden
fruit. The temptation could not have been reduced to lower
terms, and yet be a trial of obedience. We cannot discern
any thing thus far which impeaches the benevolence of God.

Now we come to consider ourselves. In consequence of
this apostasy, all the posterity of these first parents are born
with a sinful nature. To this, objection is made. Let us come
into existence, it is said, without any bias to sin, and let each
of us take his chance for himself, to stand or to fall. This
would be benevolent. Then we should agree that God is
love.

Now, without venturing, as was said before, one step into
the unfathomable abyss of speculation on the subject of moral
evil, let us simply consider whether, in view of universally
acknowledged premises, we are warranted in saying, that a
contrary method with regard to our moral probation would be
any more benevolent than that which God has adopted with
regard to man. Let us see, on the contrary, whether the
present system be not manifestly benevolent, without presum-
ing to speculate as to its being the only method which could
possibly have been adopted. It will be enough if we see that
in the present moral constitution of things with regard to our
probation, God is love.

Instead of coming into existence as now, with a fallen nature
which will inevitably develop sinfulness, and make us liable to
its fearful consequences, we might each have been born upright, free to choose for himself whether he will stand or fall.

No redemption, however, is to be provided for us in case we fall. As angels, and as men, took upon themselves the great responsibility of sinning, with all its possible consequences, so must we. Which will we do? Assume this responsibility, each for himself, with no way of recovery if we fall? or will we consent that a progenitor shall try the experiment for us, our nature be determined by the result, and redemption be provided and offered to us in case that he involves us with himself in disobedience? Our nature is the same with that of Adam; he sinned; our will is the same free will; why should we think that we should remain upright, if Adam fell? The least possible provocation to sin existed in his case; the love of God was set against an untasted fruit, his threatenings against a tempter's word that it would make him happy. A stronger inducement to remain upright, a smaller inducement to depart from God, we could not have. Now, will we take our chance, and put our condition at stake, knowing what the result of the experiment was in the case of our fellow-creature, Adam? It is no want of benevolence in God not to let men take that risk; and this is all which we seek to prove.

If angels fell, if Adam fell, for all that appears to the contrary, as many of our race would eventually have been lost as under any other moral system. It is benevolent to let men come into existence with a fallen nature, and to let this be their probation — Will you accept free forgiveness and preserving grace? You who are born in heathen lands, and have the law written in your hearts, your thoughts the meanwhile accusing or else excusing one another, your infants and young children being saved by the exercise of a compensatory dispensation toward them, and you who know good and evil, being taught by the known consequences of sin in your souls and bodies, and by the effects of doing right in an inward self-approbation, — will you accept this testimony on either side, obey, and live? And you for whom revelation is added to the light of nature, you with the gospel of Jesus Christ in your hands, will you obey the gospel, and so be saved? Motives of infinite tenderness plead with you to this effect: "for if ye do these things ye shall never fall;" but if in a state of original uprightness you sin, you sin as angels did, with no Redeemer. We may safely assert that our present condition, as fallen creatures, with a Redeemer, is, to say the least, and to speak very far within bounds, no less a proof that God is love, than angels or Adam had in being made to try the question of obedience or disobedience for themselves, with the consesequences annexed. So far as we are informed, every race of creatures is placed on probation.

If this be so, and if it would have been indispensable that every one of us should have had some trial on which his character and standing forever should depend, we cannot fail to admit that the question on which we are now tried, viz., whether we will repent and accept a free and full redemption, is as favorable and as safe for us as the question, whether we will remain upright and live, or fall and be irretrievably lost. And therefore no injury is done by making our progenitor try the question for us, and connect us with himself in his fall, and in his recovery by the infinite mercy of God. Had we fallen in Adam with no possibility of restoration, the question would be totally different from the form in which it now stands. Then it would have been, whether it is benevolent to involve a race in the doings of their progenitor, and give them no opportunity to retrieve their state. No such question is raised by the conduct of God towards us. Redemption is contemporaneous with our apostasy; they must be contemplated together; it is injustice towards God to separate them. Therefore, all the invectives against the present moral constitution of things as unjust and cruel, are themselves unfair, because they leave out of view one half of the truth; for the provision made for man's entire recovery is, to say the least, as great a proof of benevolence, as his apostasy, which involved us, could, by any misrepresentation or partial statement, be of the opposite. Hence, when we hear men say of our coming into the world with a constitutional bias towards evil, that God is a hard master, and treats us cruelly, and requires brick without straw, and sets us adrift with the chances of shipwreck all against us, we feel that extreme injustice is done to the character of the ever-blessed God. What would men have had their Maker do for them? Do they insist that he ought to have given them each a chance to test the question for himself, whether to remain upright, or to throw away his inheritance, like Satan? Is this the infinite privilege which they covet? Is God unrighteous in denying them the opportunity to draw, in that lottery, the prize of eternal life, or the blank alternative, perdition? Surely, if they reflect on the plan of mercy, which, we maintain, God has devised for us, they cannot, as men of understanding, impeach the divine benevolence; and as to its wisdom, it may be well for us to postpone our conclusions against it till we are better informed upon the question whether, in the compass of the divine knowledge, there was any other expedient which was at once so honorable to God and safe for man. But as to benevolence, there can be no reasonable denial, that the connecting of us with Adam, with the intentional provision of a Redeemer, is as kind, there is as much evidence in it of love, as in allowing angels to stand or fall each upon his own responsibility, with no provision for their recovery if they apostatized.

This view of the case is not invalidated by all the misery which sin has occasioned in the world. God is not the author of it. He makes man free, tells him what consequences will ensue upon his obedience or disobedience, and then, if by one

man sin enters into the world, and death by sin, and so death
passes upon all men, for that all have sinned, the question is,
whether this is any worse than it would have been had we
fallen without a Saviour; and whether we should have fallen
is a question whose very uncertainty is fitted to appall the
mind, and to make the absolute certainty of restoration from
a fallen state by a Redeemer, if we choose to accept it, an
object of grateful contemplation, and a proof that God is love,
seeing that he is not willing that men should perish.

Yet, it will be replied, they do perish, we are told, by mil-
lions, and they perish in consequence of their strong constitutional predisposition to sin. Now, before we suffer ourselves
to impugn the goodness of God on this score, would it not be
well to know whether or no as many would not have perished
if each had had a separate probation. Then, if liability to
fall be inseparable from every state of existence, the question
must be removed back to the very origin of all things, and we
must say, Is it right for God to create moral and accountable
beings, some of whom will voluntarily sin and be lost? He
who feels competent to be the judge of the Almighty, or even
to be his counsellor, needs at least to read once more, or perhaps for the first time, the Almighty's words to Job, on the
expediency of sitting in judgment upon the eternal purposes
of God. If it be said that such a remark is fitted to silence,
not to satisfy, it is interesting to know that God did not seek
to silence Job upon the subject, but he addresses him thus :
" Gird up now thy loins like a man, for I will demand of thee,
and answer thou me." And it is not by metaphysical questions that the Most High argues with him ; but he makes use
of the snow, and hail, and rain, and lightnings, the lion, the
raven, the wild goat, the wild ass, the unicorn, the ostrich,
the peacock, the horse, the hawk, the eagle, behemoth, and
leviathan, to show that he to whom these creatures and things

are mysteries, and more than a match for both his wisdom and his strength, while they never cease to fill him with wonder and love at the divine benevolence and skill in their formation, may safely leave some other questions, relating to things higher than eagles, and deeper than the snows and floods, to the same wisdom which he does not fail to recognize in the works of nature.

But it is said, The penalty which, it is alleged, God has annexed to disobedience, cannot be consistent with love ; for, if God knows from the beginning that a great number will sin and suffer forever, his love is not a perfect attribute, or love surely does not rule in his perfections. Some stern and unamiable principle gives its character to the Being who is willing to see a portion of his offspring miserable forever, when he could have prevented it by forbearing to bestow existence upon them.

The demand here seems to be that God shall make it impossible for any of his intelligent creatures to commit sin ; and, if he cannot do so, it is claimed that true benevolence requires him not to bring them into existence.

We will forbear to consider the question whether, in the nature of things, God could create moral beings, and yet prevent them universally from sinning ; or the question why he cannot prevent all, as well as some, from apostasy. We need not involve ourselves in the perplexities of that long-debated point ; for there is an answer to this objection which lies outside of metaphysical and theological disputes.

We have reason to believe that angels who have maintained their integrity during their probation, and that the redeemed who have finished their probationary state in this world, will be kept by the power of God unto salvation forever, and that they will " never fall." We do not know in what respects the divine influence which will keep them from falling in heaven differs from the divine influence which was extended to Adam when on probation, or why it could not have kept him from falling, (as it will keep the redeemed from apostasy,) and in perfect consistency with his own liberty. This is a region into which the human mind cannot safely enter; for it involves all those questions respecting the origin of evil which are still open questions. There is a beautiful simplicity in the manner in which the Saviour treats this subject — the origin of evil — in his parable of the tares. "So the servants of the householder came and said unto him, Sir, didst thou not sow good seed in thy field? From whence, then, hath it tares? He said unto them, *An enemy hath done this.*" This is all the explanation which divine wisdom has revealed with regard to this perplexing subject. We are left to suppose that, in order to make a universe of free minds, it is necessary that all, in some period of their existence, should be tried as to their allegiance. In saying this, we do not step beyond the bounds of revelation; for we surely know that man was thus tried, and we also know that of the angels some have fallen. Then the question would be this : Is it, after all, injustice or unkindness to wake up an immortal spirit from non-existence, endue it with godlike powers and faculties, place it under the most favorable circumstances in the immediate presence of God, and give it permission to choose life or death?

Let us apply the question to the following case, and see how we decide such questions in human affairs : A man at the head of the engraving department in the Bank of England is intrusted with great responsibilities. If faithful, he is of immense service to the community in the prevention of counterfeiting. His salary is in proportion to his great responsibilities. In his silent, quiet way, he is the means of unmeasured benefit to the commercial world; and all these considerations unite to keep him upright, while, at the same time, great watchfulnesss is exercised over him, and he feels that unsleeping vigilance marks every one of his official acts. But notwithstanding all these guards, and his powerful inducements to be honest, we will suppose that he perverts his trust, commits large forgeries, and is transported for life, to be a convict in a penal colony, making his wife a widow, his children fatherless, and covering his family and friends with a cloud of sorrow which is worse than death. Now, who will undertake to say, It is wrong to place a human being in circumstances where defalcation is possible? Who will venture the judgment that the inducements to uprightness and its great rewards are not consistent with benevolence, because, if disregarded, the consequences will be so fearful? Surely, if men should act on this principle, which they require at the hand of God, they could not even employ a clerk. There must be no responsibility, because it is capable of being perverted.

But some who will assent to this reasoning, and own that probation is reasonable and just, demur to the alleged eternal consequences of transgression under the government of God, and say, that it is not consistent with the benevolence of God that any of his subjects should be punished forever, let their transgressions be whatever they may. They adopt this principle as the foundation of every thing, even of the being and attributes of God. The ultimate, eternal happiness of every intelligent being, they say, is absolutely required by the great law of benevolence, and God can neither be nor do any thing inconsistent with this.

Let us take Satan for an illustration. Let us assert, for the sake of the argument, that Satan is to be punished without end. Now it is said, It cannot be true that "God is love," while that great spirit is suffering the vengeance of eternal fire.

To this it may be replied, Good parents punish a child so

long as he sins, let the period of transgression be as long as it may.

To flinch in the chastisement, saying, After all, it is too much to punish you so long, and to keep you from my love, while the child is as rebellious as ever, would subject the parent to contempt. So long as Satan chooses to sin, we must admit that God does right in continuing the punishment.

If Satan, during the last five or six thousand years, had chosen to repent, there has been nothing to hinder him; and no one can believe that, had he repented, God would have continued to punish him, whatever the natural consequences of his transgression might have been; for we, when forgiven, may still suffer from the natural effects, in body and mind, of our evil ways. Yet if Satan were penitent, hell would be a changed place to him; loving and fearing God, he would have verified those words which Milton puts into his mouth:—

> " The mind is its own place, and in itself
> Can make a heaven of hell, a hell of heaven."

Has not Satan had opportunity to repent? There is one part of his experience recorded in the Bible, which, we shall all agree, should have made him a good angel; and that is, his intercourse with Job. He is suffered to strip Job of every thing, and to afflict him with the severest bodily anguish which infernal ingenuity could select. Job comes forth from those trials a better man. Satan sees that there is that in God which is worthy to be loved even under chastisement, and to be preferred above possessions and children, and life itself; for, " though he slay me, yet will I trust in him." " Till I die, I will not remove mine integrity from me." But what does Satan after this? He afflicts Israel in Egypt four hundred years. He instigates Pharaoh to fight against God, and so on to King Saul, Jeroboam, Ahab, and Jezebel, " the man of sin," the slave trade, and all the barbarities of war. Thus, instead of ceasing to sin against God, he has been helping to fill the world with sin and misery. He has seen the most touching forms of goodness, vieing with the angelic beauty of his own original abode. He has seen Ignatius bare his breast to the lions in the Roman amphitheatre, Polycarp, John Huss, Lambert, Ridley, and Latimer embrace the stake; the Huguenots perishing for their religion " upon the Alpine Mountains cold; " he has seen John Bunyan bid adieu to his poor little blind child, and go into Bedford jail for twelve years for Christ's sake and the gospel's, — he has seen all this, and has not relented in his opposition to Christ. Were there any thing in love and pity to redeem the soul, he could not have lived through such scenes, and have also witnessed the times of Christ, the transactions in Gethsemane, the judgment hall, Calvary, and at the Resurrection, and the day of Pentecost, and not have been reclaimed. We should have to draw to a greater degree on fancy to invent a more favorable probation for him, than human fancy has ever yet shown itself able to depict. In addition to all this, the loss of heaven, and whatever there must have been of rigor in the sufferings of such a being as he under the mighty hand of God, must have supplied him with sufficient demonstration how fruitless it is to fight against God his Maker. Sympathy for such a being is misplaced, even though he shall forever eat the fruit of his doings.

But here is poor, frail, sinful man; — he sins away his day of grace. Shall a God of love deal thus with him?

We must all believe that in no instance will endless retributions be inflicted, if at all, on a human being, in which the justice of the infliction will not commend itself to the judgment of every benevolent mind as fully as in the case of Satan himself. But in arguing upon this subject, men love

to invent cases of extreme hardship, and then they appeal
to our sensibilities against the justice and benevolence of
God.   For example : Here, they say, is a youth about fifteen
years of age, subject to the infirmities and temptations of im-
mature life; he is not interested in religious things, yet by
no means openly vicious; he passes along heedless of the
future.   He is drowned.   There is no evidence that he feared
God, or that he had complied with the terms of salvation.
He had a very short probation.   Subtract the years of mere
childhood from the term of his life, and it seems appalling to
think of eternity deriving its hopeless character from the in-
discretions and follies of seven or eight years, and those the
most thoughtless years of life, the most unfavorable to pru-
dent consideration.   It is demanded whether we believe that
God will shut the door of mercy upon that youth forever, and
whether we deem it just to cut him off, and consign him to
hopeless woe, while a companion, who escapes death at the
same time, lives to the age of sixty, and enjoys tenfold oppor-
tunities to be saved, and thereby obtains salvation.

   The answer to this is twofold.   In the first place, We
greatly err in shutting the door of hope, ourselves, against
any sinner as a subject of repentance and faith.   Little do we
know what has taken place between the soul and God in the
apparently most hardened cases of sin, or in the most thoughtless and trifling young person, where sudden death has cut
short the day of grace.   Should all that may have transpired
in such cases be disclosed, perhaps it would have the effect to
harden others in their sin, and would lead to great presump-
tion.   A wise silence is preserved, and thus our wholesome
fears are permitted to act in deterring us from trespassing on
divine forbearance.   At the same time, no one can say what
intercourse the Spirit of God may have had with the soul in
the near approach of death, and even in cases where the

senses cannot report to the bystanders the operations of the mind. Perhaps it will not be deemed unsuitable here to say, It was not without warrant in the possibilities of divine mercy that a friend, on a certain occasion, presumingly sought to impart consolation to mourning parents, whose son, a graceless youth, was killed by being thrown from a horse. This friend succeeded in writing certain words on a plantain leaf which had grown up from the youth's grave; and the pious mother, as she was one day kneeling there, descried these words upon the leaf: —

> " Betwixt the saddle and the ground
> Was mercy asked, and pardon found."

This was easily interpreted by many as a preternatural revelation to the mother, that her child repented and found pardon through Christ in the last moments of a wicked life. No one will say that the assertion in this fraud had no warrant in the nature of things.

We charge God foolishly if we impute to him vindictive acts before we know that they have occurred.

We have another answer to the inquiry now under consideration. A young person may as intelligently and deliberately refuse the offers of eternal life, and choose to risk the consequences of eternal death, as a person of the maturest age. This is subject to the judgment of Him who " will not lay on man more than right, that he should enter into judgment with God. For the work of a man will he render unto him, and cause every man to find his own way." God can place the subject of religion before the mind of a youth with such clearness, and vividness, and persuasion; cause him to be approached and followed with such heavenly influences from every source which divine and human love can employ, and set before him the endless consequences of his conduct;

3

and the youth may deliberately reject his God and Saviour,
and make answer that he would prefer banishment from God
rather than love such a being as he clearly perceives him to
be, or to be saved in such a way as the gospel makes plain
to his understanding, — so that God will remove him from this
world, where his example and influence would corrupt many
others, and suffer him to indulge his opinions and feelings
among those of his own tastes and preferences.   How long
this sinner shall remain in this world of probation before he
is removed to a state of penal infliction, God, the Judge, will
decide.   " Shall not the Judge of all the earth do right ? "

This illustration, in some of its particulars, has been drawn
from a recent statement to the writer by a very intelligent
lady now deceased, with regard to her feelings and words
during the period of youth, when convinced of her sins and
of the way of salvation by Christ.   She told her Christian
friends that she fully understood the idea of justification by
faith, without works, through the sufferings and death of
Christ, but that she hated it with a cordial hatred; that she
never would submit to be saved in that way ; and that if
heaven was to be obtained only in that way, she would say
to God that she did not wish to have any part in his heaven,
and that he might dispose of her as he pleased.   These were
precisely her words.   It could truly be said to her, " Ye have
both seen and hated both me and my Father." There are feelings in many an unrenewed heart which do not make such
explicit and bold expression of themselves ; but many will
recognize in these words their own fearful similitude.   This
deliberate and almost impious rejection of divine wisdom and
love in Christ Jesus, did not meet with what might be deemed
its just recompense of reward ; for, by methods of gentle and
winning grace, that heart was prevailed upon to accept the
way of salvation by a Redeemer, and the penitent lived to a

good age, eminently useful in bringing souls to Christ, and in leading some to be preachers of that faith which once she destroyed. But if God had taken her at her word, and had removed her from time into eternity, leaving her to her own choice, one thing is certain, that she could never have impeached his goodness in suffering her to choose for herself, and for being willing to lie down in endless sorrow rather than to sing "forced hallelujahs" in heaven.

But now it will be said, Inasmuch as 'God was love' in thus turning her from her sin and folly, we believe that in the next world he will be the same; he will perform similar acts of grace in eternity, or we cannot believe that his character as a God of love is perfect.

The answer to this may be as follows: Whatever God might do for the recovery of the soul in the world to come, he cannot surpass that which, if we believe the gospel, he has already done to save us. This remark, it will be borne in mind, does not touch the question whether God will do any thing more hereafter to save the soul; but we may say without fear of contradiction, that nothing can exceed the incarnation of the Word, and the sufferings and death of Christ, as an expression and proof of love to sinners. If this be granted, it cannot be said that, after having bestowed the utmost proof of love on men, if God should, at a given time, cease in his efforts to reclaim them, this is a just allegation against him as wanting in perfect love. " What more could I do in my vineyard that I have not done in it?" Shall I, by omnipotent force, create grapes on vines which my sun and rain, my tillage and dressing, have failed to make fruitful?

But it may be said, God has not, in this world, tried the effect of severity to its full extent. If God is perfect in his love, he will not give over till he has used extreme measures of chastisement to save an immortal soul.

This implies that chastisement can succeed to accomplish that which infinite loving kindness has failed to do.

We have had one great experiment tried before our eyes, as to chastisement being the ultimate means of reformation, in the history of the Jews. More of them, by a hundred fold, were converted under the preaching of the gospel, apart from their, chastisements, than have been converted during their centuries of punishment. The experiment is sufficient to show that chastisement, of itself, is not "the power of God and the wisdom of God unto salvation." Christ is that "power," that "wisdom." Ages of woe, mingled with promises of restoration, have not succeeded in making the Jews submit to the Messiah. But affliction, of itself, even while holding in its hand exceeding great and precious promises, cannot reclaim the Jewish people, in a world of mercy, from their infidelity. He who believes that any process of recovery is to succeed the atonement by Christ, we will not say, gets no encouragement to his belief from the Bible, but, does infinite discredit to the atonement, as the grand and ultimate method of influencing man as a moral agent; and, if the Bible does not represent Christ and his sacrifice to be the last effort of mercy, and the rejection of him to be followed by "everlasting destruction from the presence of the Lord," and with being "unjust still," language can make no certain impressions upon the mind. Surely we may expect that the brightness of the Father's glory, and the express image of his person, would be employed hereafter to conduct whatever remedial measures might be used to recover the soul from sin; and yet it does not look like a continuation of his merciful presence and influence to say to the hopeful subjects of his continued grace, "Depart from me, ye cursed, into everlasting fire, prepared for the devil and his angels!"

Yes, "God is love," now and forever; and the darkest

parts of his system are far from countervailing the proofs of it afforded by all that we know of his ways. They who take mournful views of the present world, and of their afflicted and sinful state, should remember that, in coming into this world, we strike upon a road which proceeds from a region of blessedness, and leads to a condition of surpassing glory; but the section over which we are passing is, for wise. reasons, one of trial and sorrow. We must take into view the past and the future of the great career ; and, if we obey, we shall at last have infinite reasons for gratitude that we have been brought into being. For, if God is love, he is this to every one who is willing to love him ; and if any refuse, they have but their choice. Let the heavens, earth, and seas bring their testimonies that God is love ; let sight, and taste, and smell, and touch, all the melodies and harmonies of the world, and all the sensibilities of the soul, declare that God is love : we have in the incarnation and sacrifice of Christ a proof which exceeds them all. One of the persons in the Godhead takes the form of man, lies in the manger of Bethlehem, passes through the conditions of youth and manhood, and at last is made a sacrifice for our sins. This is, as literally as it could be, our Creator suffering in our stead. He was "made in the likeness of sinful flesh, and for sin," and "bare our sins in his own body on the tree." If we esteem it a calamity that we come into the world with a bias towards evil, he has set over against it this manifestation of infinite love towards us, so that no one need perish ; no one will perish who would not, probably, have lost his birthright had he stood for himself in some Eden, or in heaven ; for he who will not believe in and accept Jesus Christ, has no reason to think that, if made upright and placed on probation, he could have preferred the favor of God to every possible solicitation to sin, or could have resisted his desires for untasted good, more easily than

3 *

he can now resist the present poor and unsatisfying pleasures of sin, in preference to the love and service of his Redeemer.

And now, while love will lead and guide all the acts of God, we have assurance that it will not be a weak love; it can never excite the suspicion of imbecility : on the contrary, all the attributes of God are filled with love, and love is filled with all the attributes of God. If we decline the proposals which this love and wisdom make to us as intelligent and free subjects of the divine government; if we refuse to believe the simple, plain story of sin and redemption, and prefer our false philosophy ; if it must be said of us, " He feedeth on ashes ; a deceived heart hath turned him aside, so that he cannot deliver his soul, nor say, Is there not a lie in my right hand?" and so we take the risk of going into the next world without a Saviour, one thing is sure — we shall, nevertheless, be eternally the monuments of the truth that God is love. Our consciences will bear witness to it ; for we shall remember how, in our lifetime, we received our good things, and we shall perceive what good things they were, to have been created under such a dispensation as that of the gospel, with its astonishing provisions and appliances to effect our salvation and happiness ; and in our separation from those who, unlike us, chose to love and worship at a throne which is called " the throne of God and of the Lamb," we shall ourselves illustrate the love of God in not suffering the universe to present such a mingled conflict of good and evil as the world presents. " As therefore the tares are gathered and burned in the fire, so shall it be in the end of the world. The Son of man shall send forth his angels, and they shall gather out of his kingdom all things that offend, and them that do iniquity, and shall cast them into a furnace of fire ; there shall be weeping and gnashing of teeth." When a man suffers capital punishment, it is discretionary, in certain cases, for the government to give up his body to the surgeons, and so the felon subserves the purposes of science and humanity, and involuntarily helps to heal and save men. "The Lord hath made all things for himself, yea, even the wicked for the day of evil." To every soul he will say, "Friend, I do thee no wrong." He "will have all men to be saved and come to the knowledge of the truth." "As I live, saith the Lord, I have no pleasure in the death of him that dieth, but that the wicked turn and live. Turn ye, turn ye, for why will ye die, O house of Israel?" But God will eventually use all, and every thing, to glorify him. The commonwealth does not desire convicts for the sake of their manual labor, but if they make themselves felons, the state will avail itself of their handicraft.

As there is nothing which grows that affords us more pleasure than a noble vine, God selects it as an illustration of men, when they fulfil the purpose of their creation ; and if they do not, he represents them to be as useless and worthless as the wood of the vine. "Son of man, what is the vine more than any tree? Shall wood be taken thereof to do any work? Or will men take a pin of it to hang any vessel thereon? Behold, it is cast into the fire for fuel; the fire devoureth both the ends of it, and the midst of it is burned. Is it meet for any work?"[1] Thus the soul of man is capable of perpetual advancement towards God; but if it persists in sin, it is no more "meet for any work." As no good use can be made of a bad book, an obscene picture, or garments infected with contagious disease, but they must be buried or burned, so the sinner, if he cannot be reclaimed, must be disposed of in such a way as wisdom and justice shall determine. But some bestow all their sympathy on the incorrigible sinner, and forget that there are rights and privileges belonging to others — rights of protection, rights of self-defence — which, to say the least, are of equal importance with his. Others seem to make

---

[1] Ezek. xv.

small account of sin; they see no reason for future, endless
punishment, because they perceive nothing to punish. Others
seem to think of God only as of a fond parent, who has no
object but to see his children enjoy themselves, and with whom
the shutting up of one of his offspring in close confinement for
life would be impossible; and is he, they say, more humane
than God? But so long as there are such subjects as Satan
and his angels, and wicked men, to be governed, there is, of
course, a God with a character appropriate to his office as gov-
ernor of these his subjects. A man with such softness of character as many impute to the Most High, would not have the
qualifications necessary in the humblest magistrate; he could
not be trusted to try a question which involved the personal
liberty of an offender. It is enough to make one sick and
faint at heart to think of such a being as at the head of affairs.
Far different is the God whom we have, for example, in the
vision of Nahum, the Elkoshite, — in which terror and beauty
vie with each other: " God is jealous, and the Lord revengeth; the Lord revengeth, and is furious; the Lord taketh
vengeance on his adversaries, and he reserveth wrath for his
enemies. The Lord is slow to anger, and great in power, and
will not at all acquit the wicked; the Lord hath his way in
the whirlwind and in the storm, and the clouds are the dust of
his feet. Who can stand before his indignation? and who can
abide in the fierceness of his anger? His fury is poured out
like fire, and the rocks are thrown down by him. The Lord
is good, a stronghold in the day of trouble, and he knoweth
them that trust in him; but with an overrunning flood he will
make an utter end thereof, and darkness shall pursue his
enemies."

If there be such a God, and our aversion to him be owing
to any moral perversity on our part, there will be no need of
outward inflictions to make us completely wretched, so long as
we remain alienated from him. Our condition for eternity

would, therefore, be hopeless, unless in this world we should become reconciled to God; for, if this aversion is based upon any correct perception of his character, the more we know of him the more shall we desire to flee from him.

This brings us to one more proof that God is love, which must by no means be omitted. All men are by nature averse to the character and government of God, by reason of sin. This is true not only of those who by the force of education are prejudiced against what are called the evangelical doctrines, but of those also who have been taught to believe them. Every man by nature has "the carnal mind" which "is enmity against God; for it is not subject to the law of God, neither indeed can be." This aversion is criminal; yet it is such that, if left to themselves, all will, freely and wickedly, refuse to love and obey God. The fall has not impaired man's natural ability to love goodness; of course, man is capable of loving infinite goodness; but that exists in one whose will is contrary to that of the sinner, and to whose moral character the sinner, while he loves sin, has an utter distaste; so that no one can even come to Christ except the Father, which hath sent him, draw him. In this direful predicament, God interposes, and overcomes the sinful reluctance of some; and still the invitation is, "Whosoever will, let him take the water of life freely;" but while many refuse, others are persuaded and enabled to embrace Jesus Christ as he is freely offered in the gospel. They then experience that new birth which is the special work of the Holy Spirit. It will seem superfluous to some that it should be said, that whoever, for example, is reading these lines is as welcome to all the blessings of the gospel as any other. No secret decree prevents him from obtaining the full benefits of salvation by Christ. No abuse of privileges, no rejection of offered mercy, no hard thoughts, nor unjust accusations, of his Maker, nor even blasphemous words against him, have shut the door of mercy

upon his soul. He who, for his sake, lay in the manger at
Bethlehem, and expired on the cross, is now his advocate on
high, and as a fruit of his merits, the Holy Spirit strives to
bring the soul to God. Let him reflect how marked the dealings of God have been with him, in his preservations, blessings, and trials, and in the means employed to keep him back
from presumptuous faults, and to bring his attention again and
again to the subject of religion; let him consider, if, in all
this, there be not some appearance of a desire to effect his
salvation, and that, too, notwithstanding great provocations to
give him up forever. Is there any love like this? Not only
in the ransom paid for us, but in the persevering efforts of
injured mercy, in behalf of every one of us, there are proofs
that God is love which will furnish us with our principal testimony to that truth.

It may, therefore, be said to every one, let his character be
as it may, God loves you. Complacency in us while we are
wicked, of course, he cannot feel; but there are feelings of
love on the part of God towards every one, such as are not
equalled by any human interest in the object of its good will.
While the displeasure of God against sin, and the necessity
of its endless punishment, are fundamental truths, God is
love; hell is not the exponent of his character; it is a sub-
sidiary in his administration; but as Gehenna did not lie
where the Temple, " beautiful for situation, the joy of the
whole earth, on the sides of the north," was built, so the fore-
most object in the Deity is not wrath, nor punishment. But
when Moses prayed, " I beseech thee show me thy glory," the
Lord said, " I will make all my goodness pass before thee ; "
yet it is to be noticed that he immediately adds, And I " will
be gracious to whom I will be gracious, and will show mercy
on whom I will show mercy ; " — in which expressions we see
that while grace and mercy are set forth to make the chief
impressions of the divine character, they are enunciated in a

way to suggest the idea of discrimination in the manner in which they are exercised. And so when, on Sinai, God proclaimed his name at the renewal of the tables of stone, it was "the Lord God, merciful and gracious, long suffering, and abundant in goodness and truth, keeping mercy for thousands, forgiving iniquity, and transgression, and sin, visiting the iniquity of the fathers upon the children, and upon the children's children, unto the third and to the fourth generation." Here the predominant impression is that of goodness; yet the very term "*long-suffering*" suggests that there are bounds to mercy, while the avowed principle of connecting parents and children, as here described, makes one feel that the character of God has depths in it which are not all explored, nor sounded, by the analogy of earthly parentage. If we leave out any essential attribute from the character of God, we do not worship the true God. At the same time, there is an order and a proportion, in those attributes, to disregard which is like applying the wrong end of a magnet for a given purpose. As we are sinners, all the attributes of God have relation to us; and hence it is that redemption, unfolding all those attributes in their various exercise, and in disclosing to us, as it were by necessity, the mystery in the divine nature of Father, Son, and Holy Ghost, is represented as the chief work of Jehovah.

Each of us is urged to be a subject of that redemption, and to afford an illustration of the attributes of God in our salvation, and not in our future, endless punishment. "For God so loved the world, that he gave his only begotten Son, that whosoever believeth in him should not perish, but have everlasting life. FOR GOD SENT NOT HIS SON INTO THE WORLD TO CONDEMN THE WORLD, BUT THAT THE WORLD THROUGH HIM MIGHT BE SAVED."

APPENDIX.

BRIEF NOTICE

OF

REV. T. STARR KING'S "TWO DISCOURSES," ETC.[1]

THE circumstances under which the discourse, of which the present pages are a supplement, was preached, are generally known. They are stated in the 'Correspondence' prefixed to it, in the first number of this series. After the additional statement, in these pages, of the writer's views concerning the character of God, as concerned in the moral condition and destinies of our race, very little needs to be added on this point, in this brief notice of the "Two Discourses" recently published by the Pastor of Hollis Street Church, in reply to the first sermon on this subject. The present publication ('God is Love') had its origin as a sermon not in consequence of these "Two Discourses," (which, if preached, had not then been published,) but from the desire of the author to lay before his stated hearers a somewhat more completed view of the important theme.

While no complaint is here made, and no objection is felt that the Pastor of the Hollis Street Church should have replied, as he did, to the sermon above named, or that he should have published his answer, yet, as the invitation to preach contained no intimation of a purpose to use the sermon in aid of a counter statement of doctrinal opinions on the same subject, the present occasion may fairly be used to say a few words in reply. Perhaps the apprehension that there would be any occasion to say them, might have operated as a reason to decline the courteous and fair invitation to preach. And now, in the same friendly spirit which led to the acceptance of the invitation, and which, it was apparent, dictated it, all that shall be said will be in no controversial spirit, but with a sincere and earnest desire to commend our evangelical views still further to the understandings and hearts of others.

---

[1] "The Doctrine of Endless Punishment for the Sins of this Life, unchristian and unreasonable. Two Discourses, delivered in Hollis Street Church. By Rev. Thomas Starr King. Boston: Crosby, Nichols & Co."

(36)

The thought that the discourse on the "Reasonableness," &c., may have led the author of the "Two Discourses" to say certain things, which will be quoted, awakens a natural and a friendly feeling of responsibleness in him who may have been the occasion of such utterances. This makes him more ready to say a few words in reply.

It is a remark of Bucholtzer, "A preacher is known by his peroration." There, his heart, his motive, his governing purpose, appear. He has ceased to argue; he appeals; and the controlling emotions of his soul are then, to his thoughts and feelings, like the push of the sea which sends the waves ashore. It was, therefore, with the deepest interest, and with feelings which cannot be fully expressed, that the closing paragraph but one of the "Two Discourses" was perused. It is as follows : —

"Brethren, we need a religion that shall have no fear of the justice of God forever, but boundless confidence in it, rather. It is heathen to ask for an interest in Christ, in order to be shielded from God's law. If you are a sinner, seek deliverance from yourself, but not from God's law, or from God. Face his law. Ask for its searchings and scourge. Even if you are about to die, be not afraid of infinite justice. To slip away from it would be your only danger. It is inseparably mixed with God's love, as the gravitation of the sun with its light and heat."

The thought that these words were addressed to a company of immortal beings, each of whom, with us, is to meet a dying hour, and then is to answer for the deeds done in the body; and the recollection of those explicit words, "Therefore by the deeds of the law shall no flesh be justified in his sight;" "to declare, I say, at this time, his righteousness, that he might be just and the justifier of him that believeth in Jesus;" and how the very chiefest of the apostles counted every thing but dung, that he might "win Christ, and be found in him, not having," he says, "mine own righteousness, which is of the law, *but that which is through the faith of Christ*, the righteousness which is of God by faith;" and moreover, the thought that the speaker himself, with us, will one day test the correctness of these words, in their application to himself, — awakens a feeling of unaffected interest toward all who believe and speak these things; and yet it is an interest which the proprieties of life forbid us to express, save in the guarded manner of deference to the right of private judgment, and of respect for individual responsibleness. No words from human lips, on this theme, ever seemed so bold as these. They call up, vividly, the image of a man leaping the enclosures of Sinai, venturing into the darkness and tempest which were round about God, and, without availing himself

4

even of the mediatorship of Moses, protesting, ' I want no mediator,' and beckoning his tribe in Israel to follow him ; — although Moses himself had said, " I exceedingly fear and quake."

The innumerable souls which have fled for refuge from the law of God to Him " who is the end of the law for righteousness to every one that believeth," cannot have been deceived in the expressions which divine revelation made upon them ; for they are the great body of devout persons in all ages. We have no hymns in our language which celebrate the justice of God as the foundation of a sinner's hope. Never do we hear men of devout lives saying, in health or in sickness, ' God forbid that I should glory save in the justice of God.' He explicitly tells us in his word that we have no righteousness of our own ; hence we have no peace with God till we are justified, by his righteousness, through Christ ; and therefore it is only at the cross of Christ that, for us, " righteousness and peace have kissed each other."

The grand secret of the unbelief here expressed with regard to the way of salvation by faith, appears in these words, in another part of these " Two Discourses." Speaking of the statement commonly made, that the doctrine of future, endless retribution is inseparably intertwined with the Supreme Deity of Christ, the preacher says, (p. 60,) —

" Brethren, I do not believe in the Supreme Deity of Christ, or that it is taught in any portion of the New Testament. I know that most of the noblest Christians of the world to-day do believe it. But," &c.

This being so, and while it is so, nothing else which pertains essentially to the great system of revealed truth, as evangelical believers hold it, is ever truly received. If Jesus Christ is a foundation stone, the superstructure will correspond to his nature and character. If he be " the Word who was with God and who was God," there must be an infinite difference between all which he does and that which a creature can do. The sufferings and death of such a person as Christ, in whom the divine Word is incarnate, are, by an immeasurable difference, of more consequence than the sufferings and death of a created being. Accordingly we find a stress laid on the death of Christ which is fully accounted for, as we believe, only in there being a propitiation for sin. Perhaps the author of the " Two Discourses " was present with some ministerial friends when one, formerly a minister of like views with him, and now a distinguished ornament in the literary world, remonstrated with them for making use of the Lord's Supper, because of its absolutely sacrificial associations ; alleging that a principal reason with him for leaving the ministry was, the necessity of using that ordinance, when he utterly repudiated the idea of vicarious sacrifice in the death of Christ. He was, at least, consistent; his witness is true.

But the author continues his objections to the idea that the atonement involves the doctrine of future, endless retribution; and he asks, (p. 61,) —

"Why must the possibility of pardon stop at the grave? Why, if a soul can be saved from just wrath here, through faith in the atonement, cannot a like faith avail, if a sinner offers it who has suffered for centuries in the abyss?"

Such a question — and it is one of fearful interest — must be referred for the only answer, if any, which can be given, to the revelation of God. As man did not fix the way and the terms of salvation, he can himself give no satisfactory answer to this inquiry. How long probation shall be, is determined only by infinite wisdom. In proportion to the stupendous sacrifice made for sin, it may be that the term during which it shall be offered is made brief. This seems to be hinted at here: "He that despised Moses' law died without mercy, under two or three witnesses. Of how much sorer punishment, suppose ye, shall he be thought worthy who has trodden under foot the Son of God, and counted the blood of the covenant wherewith he was sanctified an unholy thing, and hath done despite unto the Spirit of grace? For we know Him that hath said, Vengeance belongeth unto me; I will recompense, saith the Lord." These are singular words; they relate to the rejection of mercy through the blood of Christ; and the "vengeance" and "recompense" spoken of, imply other attributes and feelings in God than those of a father. When we think of probation as being short, compared with eternity, we are to remember what the offer is, who makes it, and by what means it was procured. True, it is but a little while, at the longest, that any of us live in the world; but, during that brief space of time, proposals are made to us by our God, in our own nature, from an atoning cross; and a very few, intelligent, deliberate acts of rejecting or neglecting those proposals, have an importance proportioned to the nature of the proposals; hence it is said, "How shall we escape if we neglect so great salvation?" We who have fully known the way of pardon by a Saviour's death, may not properly ask why we may not avail ourselves of the same offer ages hence.

The author tells us, (p. 59,) that

"The doctrine [of endless retribution] is a fiction, an invention, pure and simple, so far as the Old Testament is concerned." — "There are not any disclosures about the details or destinies of a future life in any book

written between the time of Adam and Malachi. The idea of eternal pun‚
ishment came into the Jewish mind and literature from heathen sources."

There is no room here to enter fully into an exhibition of the
manner in which the idea of future and final retribution is interwoven
with the whole of the Old Testament history, from the time when it
was said to Adam, "In the day that thou eatest thereof, thou shalt
surely die." Nor is it necessary to pursue the illustration of this
truth, seeing that we have a certain testimony upon the point which
it will be hard for any to set aside. — The statement is, that the
Old Testament nowhere teaches the doctrine of future, endless
punishment.

The rich man in hell was told that between him and heaven there
was a great gulf fixed, "so that they which would pass from hence
to you cannot; neither can they pass to us, that would come from
thence."

"Then he said, I pray thee, therefore, father, that thou wouldest
send him to my father's house; for I have five brethren; that he may
testify unto them, lest they also come into this place of torment."

Now let us attentively consider the reply which Abraham made to
this proposal: "Abraham saith unto him, They have Moses and the
prophets; let them hear them."

We do not then hear the rich man reply, Nay, father Abraham;
thou knowest that there is not in the Old Testament one word from
Moses to Malachi relating to this hopeless misery.

The opportunity thus to impugn the Old Testament was not
embraced. The reply of the rich man simply was, "Nay, father
Abraham, but if one went unto them from the dead, they will
repent."

Then follow those words which stamp the seal of heaven, by the
hand of Jesus Christ, upon the Old Testament, as a sufficient guide
to the men who possessed it, with respect to eternity: "And he said
unto him, If they hear not Moses and the prophets, neither will they
be persuaded though one rose from the dead."

All this should awaken in us a candid desire to find those testimonies in the Old Testament to future retributions — testimonies which
even a messenger from the other world, it seems, could not make
more convincing. Wherever and whatever the rich man was suffering,
his surviving Jewish brethren had, in their Old Testament Scriptures
all the information which a spirit from within the veil could usefully
impart.

The objection perhaps most commonly urged against future, endless retribution is set forth in these Discourses, with the aid of a quotation from an eminent writer and preacher of the same faith with our author. The slight impression and influence which, it is said, the doctrine has upon those who believe it, is used to show that

" ' It may be a sort of theory to be speculated about, to be coldly believed in, but it is not truth that can be taken home to the heart. *Coldly* believed in, did we say? No; so believed, it is not believed in at all. It is not *believed*, unless it is believed in horror and anguish; unless it sends its votary to his nightly pillow in tears, and wakes him every morning to sorrow, and carries him through every day burdened as with a world's calamity, and hurries him, worn out with apprehension and pity, to a premature grave. He who should grow sleek and fat, and look fair and bright, in a prison from which his companions were taken one by one, day by day, to the scaffold and the gibbet, could make a far better plea for himself than a good man living and thriving in this dungeon world, and believing that thousands and thousands of his fellow-prisoners are dropping daily into everlasting burnings.' " [1]

To allude once more to Rev. John Foster's thoughts on this subject, we find him also dwelling with much force on this same objection — that it " sits so easy on the minds of the religious and benevolent believers of it." " If the tremendous doctrine be true, it ought to be continually proclaimed as with the blast of a trumpet, inculcated and reiterated with ardent passion, in every possible form of illustration; no remission of the alarm to the thoughtless spirits." " The most prolonged thundering alarm is but as the note of an infant, a bird, or an insect, in proportion to the horrible urgency of the case."

What, then, we might ask, can we possibly do, which will be at all proportioned to the urgency of the case, even if we should live in a frenzy, and cry out perpetually, as the people in the flood must have done, to one another? — In all these strictures, in the first place, there is not a just consideration of the principles of the human mind as susceptible to moral suasion. In waking a sleeper from a burning dwelling, we may adopt measures to rouse and save him, which would only disgust a sinner if applied to his moral sensibilities. Clamor and cries of distress, tones of sorrow inarticulate through grief, a countenance on which unutterable concern for the perishing should always be depicted, would fail of their benevolent intention, if employed, Sabbath after Sabbath, and from day to day, by preachers of the gospel to save men. Christ and the apostles were plain and bold

---

[1] " Two Discourses," pp. 63, 64. — Quoted from Rev. Dr. Dewey.

in their warnings; but they understood human nature too well to scream their admonitions, or to use the intonations of the affrighted.[1]

But, further, these strictures are not in accordance with our general conduct in other things. We are all aware that scenes of indescribable wretchedness exist in this city, perhaps not far from our dwellings. This knowledge does not keep the most humane among us agitated, as it is sometimes demanded that we should be, if we believe in future punishment. Human nature could not endure such excitement where no help could be rendered. Our various duties would forbid it.

No minister of Christ, and no believer in the punishment of the wicked, will fail to confess, with shame and sorrow, that he feels so little the power of this belief; that it influences his feelings in so small a measure. But he will make the same confessions with regard to his conceptions of the Saviour's love, the evil of sin, and the blessedness of heaven.

But there is a singular inconsistency in those who make this objection to a belief in future punishment. A pamphlet was published in this city several years ago, in which the writer dwelt at large on this objection, quoting Mr. Foster, and expatiating at length on the argument. Then, strange to say, in another part of his work, and in seeming forgetfulness of all this, he compiled two pages, in small type, of fearful representations respecting future punishment, from some of the American Tract Society's publications, — Baxter's Call to the Unconverted, Alleine's Alarm, Saurin, President Edwards, and the Peep of Day; and, in questionable taste, he called this "Hellomania." Some men, surely, according to his own showing, have cleared their skirts of the blood of souls; even Mr. Foster would nave admitted this, could he have perused that fearful emblazonry of the terrors of the Lord. But it seems hard to be reproached by the same individuals, with unreasonable apathy with regard to future punishment, and then to have them utter epithets against us, which seem almost intolerant, for using such terrific representations of the future. Our friend, the author of the "Two Discourses," has unconsciously fallen into this inconsistency. On the sixty-third page, he has, with the concurrence of a distinguished writer, just quoted, represented us as utterly deceived in believing as we profess to do, because we are not more in earnest in our tones and efforts. And yet,

---

[1] A distinguished physician of Boston says, that a gentleman once came into his office, and said, " Sir, I am very deaf, indeed; and now I wish you to speak slow, and low, and I can hear you."

on the fifty-second page, he had made severe strictures on a passage from the sermon on "The Reasonableness," &c., which makes the supposition that it will be wretchedness enough hereafter for sinners merely to have their own way. He quotes as follows : —

"God may say, This I will do. I will place all of you who sin, in a world by yourselves, from which I and my friends will forever withdraw. . . . . . He would take away, we must suppose, all their domestic relations, friendships, social pleasures, books, every pursuit of knowledge, music, travels, quiet sleep, morning and evening salutations.of loved ones."[1]

Then our friend exclaims, "All this forever! All this in a world devised by the infinite intellect with exquisite relation to purposes of torture !" &c.

What shall we do ? We are like "children sitting in the markets and calling unto their fellows, and saying, We have piped unto you, and ye have not danced; we have mourned unto you, and ye have not lamented." If we are mild in our persuasives, we are insincere ; if bold and startling, we shock the sense of our friends, and excite invectives against ourselves not surpassed in terror by President Edwards's sentences, nor by Alleine's Alarm. — But we must bring a charge against these same friends of ours, for their inconsistency with their own belief, in not perpetually denouncing us, and saying to their hearers concerning us, " Save yourselves from this untoward generation " — these calumniators of the most High, these tormentors before the time, and without the least warrant, of innocent men, women, and children, by their ' unchristian ' doctrine of future woe. O, how do we deserve to be driven out from among God's children into dry places, to cry and cut ourselves with stones, if all which is sometimes said of our belief is true. Where is the zeal of the unbelievers ? Our dogma " sits too easily " upon them ; they are not half awake ; may we be excused if we say, Cry louder; quit yourselves like men, till this direful faith in future retribution is banished from the world. Else allow that we are, alike, naturally incapable of responding, as we should do, to the great, awakening truths of eternity.

It seems useless to quote the names of certain distinguished men and women as having wavered in their faith about this doctrine. It is only to be wondered at, that, with so much in it to try their confidence in it as a matter of pure revelation, thousands instead of tens, among evangelical believers, do not hesitate to receive it. The overwhelming majority of devout readers find the doctrine not merely

1 " The Reasonableness," &c., p. 22.

in certain proof texts, but in the drift of Scripture, its implications, and in its fearful silence about any future state of probation.

Indeed, it admits of a question, whether, as a general thing, the most convincing proofs in the Bible of this doctrine, are not those which may be called incidental. These might fill a volume. For example, to quote from memory, " In the place where the tree falleth, there it shall lie ; " " I will laugh at your calamity, I will mock when your fear cometh ; " " the wicked shall be turned into hell ; " "as the chaff which the wind driveth away ; " " son of perdition ; " "perish ; " " shall not see life ; " " good for that man if he had not been born ; " "every tree which bringeth not forth good fruit is hewn down and cast into the fire ; " — and the implications in the parables — " shall be taken away even that which he hath ; " and the parable of the net — where the bad fishes, when drawn ashore, are not carefully thrown back into the sea, but are " cast away ; " and in the parable of the tares, which are " gathered and burned in the fire." " So shall it be in the end of this world."

It is interesting to know that evangelical men, who, from time to time, have expressed doubts or difficulties with respect to the eternity of future punishment, often admit that the Scriptures are probably against them. Mr. Foster is an illustration. A more striking case is that of Dr. Thomas Burnett, one of the twelve or fifteen quoted by our author as having denied, or doubted, this article of faith. Dr. Burnett says, " Human nature shrinks back from the very name of eternal punishment. *Yet the Scriptures seem to hold the other side.*" [1] This good man wrote in Latin against future, endless punishment, and protested against his book being translated, for the reason that men are hardly restrained, even by the fears of eternal punishment, from going into all manner of sin, and the general disbelief of the doctrine, he feared, would tend to immorality. Origen, a disbeliever in the doctrine, intimates the same thing.[2] Surely, if the Scriptures and morality are on the side of the doctrine, it is hardly " unchristian and unreasonable." [3]

---

[1] " Natura humana abhorret ab ipso nomine poenarum aeternarum, &c. At Scriptura Sacra a partibus contrariis stare videtur." — *De Statu Mort. et Résurg.* p. 288, 2d ed.

[2] Contra Celsum, lib. vi. p. 292. — Ed. Spencer.

[3] Bishop Bull, also, makes a remark on Purgatory, which applies well to the doctrine of Restoration, as injurious to morals. He calls the doctrine of Purgatory " a gross imposition, that hath been, I am persuaded, the eternal ruin of thousands of souls for whom our Lord shed his most precious blood, who

The words "*everlasting*" and "*forever*," in Scripture, do not always mean *without end.* All admit this. "The *everlasting* hills," "he shall be his servant *forever*," and many such expressions, show, that the words indicate a duration corresponding to the nature of the object, or subject. Every intelligent reader knows this.

But there is such a thing, such an idea, as *having no end;* there is a proper *eternity.* Of course, there are words to express the idea. This is certain — the same word is used to denote the duration of punishment, which conveys the idea of the only proper eternity of which the Bible speaks.[1]

But as to *Gehenna,* Dr. George Campbell says, —

"That *Gehenna* is employed in the New Testament to denote the place of future punishment prepared for the devil and his angels, is indisputable. It occurs just twelve times. In ten of these there can be no doubt; in the other two, where the expression is figurative, 'child of hell,' and 'set on fire of hell,' it will scarcely admit of a question that the figure is taken from that state of misery which awaits the impenitent.[2] These two cannot be considered as exceptions, it being the manifest intention of the writers in both cases to draw an illustration of the subject from that state of perfect wretchedness."

Our author's objection to there being any *place* called *hell,* is the common one, and he thus expresses it : —

"One cannot easily see how the word [Gehenna, or the valley of Hinnom] could pass completely over from an uncertain to a technical sense, so long as the Jewish state remained, and the polluted valley was there, shedding its historic and moral associations into the mind of the people of Palestine. After the destruction of Jerusalem, the word could become unfixed from all geographical restraints and capabilities, and wither *up* into a dry, Rabbinic designation of a place of torment in the future world." — p. 23.

The idea is this : *Gehenna* could not, to the Jewish mind, in the Saviour's days, have meant an unseen place of torment, because it was

might have escaped hell, if they had not trusted to a Purgatory." — English Works, vol. i. p. 115.

[1] Some inquire, why, in the last verse of the 25th of Matthew, we read, "*everlasting* punishment," and "life *eternal*," when one and the same Greek word, it is said, is used in both parts of the verse. It is because the translators preferred to use variety, rather than repeat the same word in a brief space. The same thing is done in John iii. 15, 16 : "That whosoever believeth in him should not perish, but have *eternal* life. For God so loved the world, that he gave his only-begotten Son, that whosoever believeth in him should not perish, but have *everlasting* life." The same Greek word is here translated by two different English words ; and this Greek word is that which is translated *everlasting*, in connection with the punishment of the wicked.

[2] Prelim. Dissert. vi. part 2.

known that *Gehenna* literally meant that noisome valley near Jerusalem; but, in after years, the term may have come into use; but it could not have done so while the people saw the smoke ascending continually.

A complete answer to this is found in the fact that Jerusalem itself gave its name to heaven: " *Jerusalem,* which is from above" — " the heavenly *Jerusalem,*" &c. Lapse of time was not necessary to grow the moss of sanctity over it, and thereby make it a synonyme for heaven. We have abundant illustrations of the immediate transferrence óf a name of a place, or thing, into the current phraseology of the people then living, to represent something in morals or life. *Billingsgate, Coventry,* to mention no others, are familiar instances.

But if the word was actually used ten or twelve times in the New Testament to denote, as we must all confess, something besides the literal valley of Hinnom, this disproves our author's theory; whether it was *hell,* or any thing else, which the word meant, in those passages, so long as it did not mean *the place outside of Jerusalem,* our author's reasoning fails. And that it did not mean that literal valley, in these cases, is perfectly clear; for one who should say to his brother, Thou fool, was not cast into *the valley of Hinnom.* God would not " destroy both soul and body " *in the valley of Hinnom;* nor were the Pharisees concerned to " escape the damnation of" *that valley.* Hence, Gehenna had, in the Saviour's time, given its name to some other place; — and where was it?

Our author tells us, —

"There is no doubt that the Pharisees of the New Testament times believed in eternal damnation. Let the doctrine receive all the strength and respectability which such an indorsement can confer." — p. 23.

Great importance belongs to this admission, which is not in the least diminished by the connection of the truth involved in it with such bad men as the Pharisees. The great Teacher uttered his woes against them for their errors; but, had Jesus been a preacher of universal salvation, what awful reproofs would they have had from him for so libelling the " infinite Father " as to teach eternal damnation! Not a word of this, however; on the contrary, he charged them with making their proselyte " twofold more a child of *Gehenna* than " themselves. This, from the lips of Him who was at that moment reprobating their errors before the people; but he did not say a word against their belief in eternal damnation as being " *unchristian* and *unreasonable.*"

But the limits of these pages forbid more extended remarks. In these "Two Discourses" we have the theory laid down that the ultimate, perfect, and eternal happiness of every intelligent creature is the first great law of the universe. To that idea the Bible must conform. "Jesus was a poet;" and all his imagery of punishment means nothing more than wholesome discipline; and Milton and Shakspeare are quoted to prove and illustrate the nature of the Saviour's figures of speech. There is no system of truth, so called, in the Bible; "asterisks," largely sprinkled in the pages of the Saviour's words, would properly express his elliptical way of communicating truth; and the apostles are less systematic than Christ. The Bible, we should judge, in our friend's view, is a glorious discharge of brilliancy, such as we see in the "golden rain," or the flight of several hundred "serpents" at once, in the pyrotechnic display; or like the sudden uprising together of a whole forest of birds, of all plumages and songs. Every thing is for intellectual and moral excitation, but fragmentary, and it cannot be pushed into a theory; nothing is very certain, except that all is to be well. God, Christ, heaven, hell, the Bible, human life, accidents, pain, death, every thing, is, each and all, subservient to this primal law of existence — the eternal happiness of angels, men, and devils. Judas, we should infer, is, just now, and perhaps is to be for a long time, rather a bad piece of statuary marble; he requires exceeding great labor to chisel off from his unpromising outside the veins and soft spots; but he is good at the centre; and Judas will yet come out an ornament to the society of heaven. It will therefore be good for that man, eventually, to have been born. As for Satan, there is probably no such being; he and his hell are Oriental metaphors. In the great sweep of ages, sin and sinners will exist only in history.

We shall, every one of us, somewhere, both preachers and hearers, forever have personal experience of the truth or error of these views. As we open the Book of Chronicles, for example, and in its lists of names, the eye rests on one — let it be *Adbeel*, — it is interesting to reflect that he, an immortal spirit, is this day pursuing his deathless career, with a personal history infinitely precious and important to him. So with each of us. It is a cause of gratefulness, therefore, to find one's self on that side of a question like this where, even if it be the wrong side, we are safe, according to the opposite theory. Great obligations are upon us who believe these momentous things. One is, not to be lofty or repulsive towards others, but to remember that our word is called the word of 'reconciliation.' And while we preach endless punishment, salvation from it, through a Redeemer, is to be our great theme. Hope does more to save men, if Christ be set forth as the ground of it, than wrath. If we believe more than others, if we receive what we deem 'the whole counsel of God,' we should ponder our steps, lest, after having believed, and especially having preached, such things, we should only have sealed our own hopeless doom. Let those of us who preach these truths, therefore, make full proof of our ministry. We are, every Sabbath, helping to save men from the wrath to come, or causing them to be without excuse, if they perish forever. "AND WHO IS SUFFICIENT FOR THESE THINGS?"